GRAPHIC NATURAL DISASTERS

TORNADOES & SUPERSTORMS

by Gary Jeffrey

illustrated by Terry Riley

The Rosen Publishing Group, Inc., New York

Published in 2007 by The Rosen Publishing Group, Inc.
29 East 21st Street, New York, NY 10010

First edition, 2007

Designed and produced by
David West Books

Editor: Gail Bushnell

Photo credits:
p4t&b,6m, NOAA Photo Library, NOAA Central Library; OAR/ERL/National Severe Storms Laboratory (NSSL); p5t, Historic NWS Collection (Photographer: Mr. Paul Huffman); p5b, Historic NWS Collection; p6t, NOAA Historical Photo Collection (Photographer: Elizabeth A. Hobbs); p6b, U.S.Coast Guard; p7t, NOAA/National Climatic Data Center; p44/45all, NOAA Photo Library, NOAA Central Library; OAR/ERL/National Severe Storms Laboratory (NSSL);

Library of Congress Cataloging-in-Publication Data

Jeffrey, Gary.
Tornadoes & superstorms / by Gary Jeffrey ; illustrated by Terry Riley.
p. cm. -- (Graphic natural disasters)
Includes index.
ISBN-13: 978-1-4042-1993-9 (library binding)
ISBN-10: 1-4042-1993-5 (library binding)
ISBN-13: 978-1-4042-1986-1 (6 pack)
ISBN-10: 1-4042-1986-2 (6 pack)
ISBN-13: 978-1-4042-1985-4 (pbk.)
ISBN-10: 1-4042-1985-4 (pbk.)
1. Tornadoes--Juvenile literature. 2. Storms--Juvenile literature.
I. Riley, Terry, ill. II. Title. III. Title: Tornadoes and superstorms.
QC955.2.J44 2007
551.55'3--dc22

2006027018

Manufactured in China

CONTENTS

TORNADOES

Tornadoes can occur all over the world, but they are most frequent in the United States, where some 1,000 tornadoes touch down every year. They cause death and around $850 million of damage.

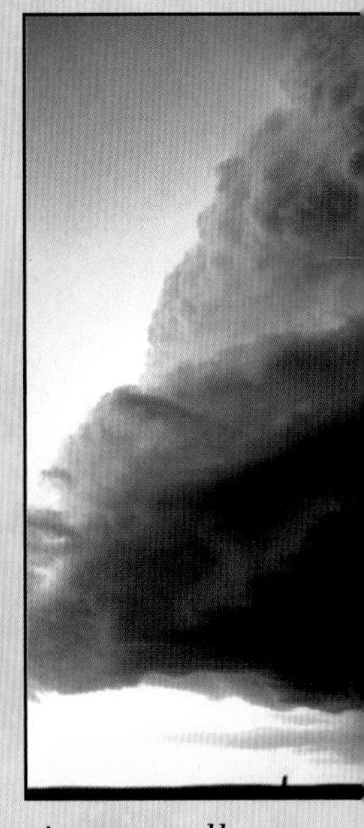

A supercell thunderstorm cloud develops (above). Rain and hail fall from the base at the front of the cloud. Behind these downpours, a tornado (below) may develop.

SUPERCELLS

A tornado is the rotating funnel cloud that reaches from the base of a supercell thunderstorm cloud to the ground. These have a very clear shape with a flat top that spreads out, called the anvil. They form when a mass of warm, humid air meets a mass of cold, dry air. Horizontal winds moving in different directions and at different heights can form rotating winds within the supercell. This is called a mesocyclone. Strong updrafts lift the rotating winds upward. As they get higher they stretch and tighten, making them spin faster. As the rotating winds hit the ground they suck up soil and debris which can color the funnel cloud or tornado. Wind speeds in tornadoes can reach over 300 mph (483 km/h), although only one in fifty have wind speeds greater than 200 mph (322 km/h). These are the F4 and F5 category tornadoes.

THE FUJITA SCALE

The strength of a tornado is measured by the Fujita scale. The scale is divided into levels ranging from F0—Gale tornado—40–72 mph (64–116 km/h) to F6—Inconceivable tornado—with wind speeds between 319 and 379 mph (513 and 610 km/h.

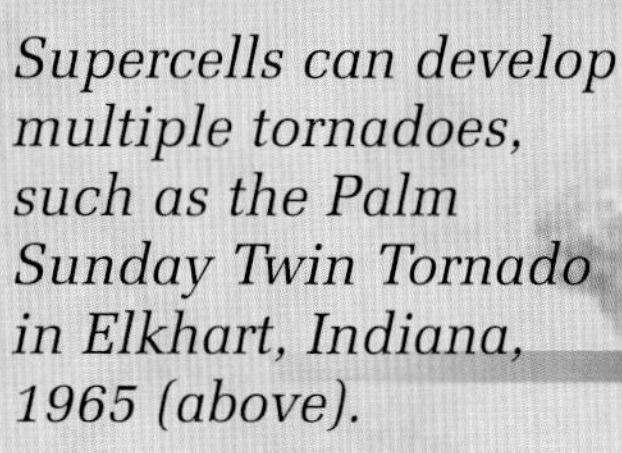

Supercells can develop multiple tornadoes, such as the Palm Sunday Twin Tornado in Elkhart, Indiana, 1965 (above).

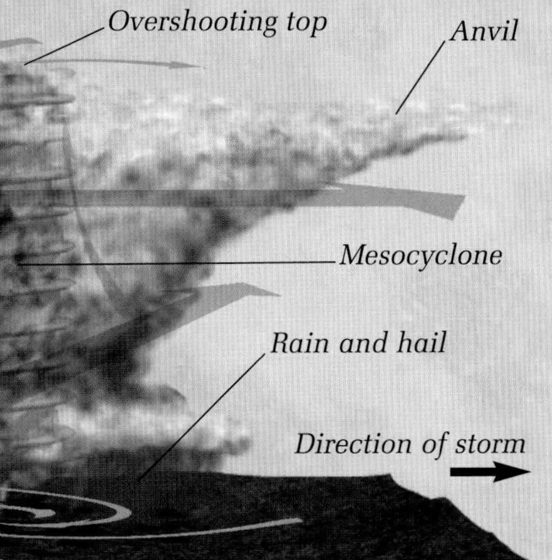

The cutaway artwork (above) shows the main parts and wind movements of a tornado-generating, supercell thunderstorm cloud.

Much of a tornado's destructive force comes from high-speed flying objects. A plastic record stuck in a telegraph pole (left) provides evidence of this power.

SUPERSTORMS

In 1993 an unusually huge and violent storm raged across eastern Canada and the East Coast of the U.S. for three days. It was called a superstorm. Since then, this word has been used to describe highly powerful storms, including cyclonic storms, nor'easters, and multiple tornadoes.

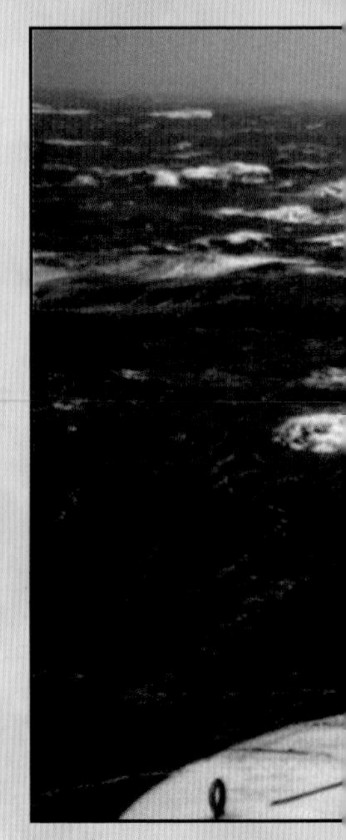

CYCLONE

This is a rotation of a mass of air around an area of low atmospheric pressure. Hurricanes and typhoons are intense tropical cyclones, but cyclones can form in the cooler mid-latitudes. These mid-latitude cyclones occur when a mass of cool air meets a mass of warm, moist air over the ocean.

NOR'EASTER

During the early winter months cold air masses develop over Canada and envelop the American Midwest, while, to the east, over the Atlantic, hurricanes sometimes form. The clash between the two air masses results in massive storms off the East Coast of the United States, and are called "nor'easters." Weather conditions include strong winds and heavy rainfall, which results in flooding, hail, snow blizzards, ice storms, high waves, and storm surges.

LANDFALL

Superstorms over the ocean generally remain there and eventually die out. Occasionally they make landfall and it is then that their violence wreaks havoc, causing loss of life and millions of dollars of damage.

The March 1993 superstorm (right) known as the "Storm of the Century" started as a cyclone in the Gulf of Mexico. It headed northeast up the East Coast of the U.S., spawning 27 tornadoes along the way. Record levels of wind strength and snowfall (left) were recorded. In all, 270 deaths and up to $6 billion dollars in damage were attributed to the storm.

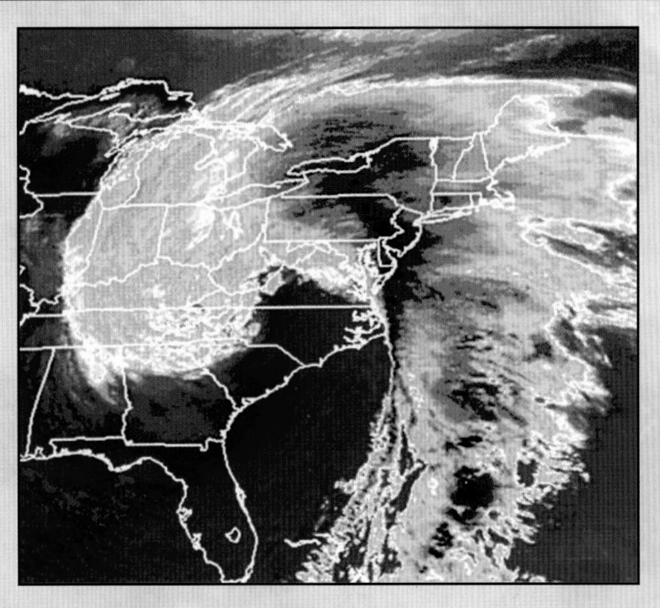

The sailing vessel Satori *flounders in heavy seas during the Halloween storm, October 30, 1991 (below). All three crew aboard were saved by the Coast Guard helicopter. Also called the "Perfect Storm," it was the result of hurricane Grace merging with an extratropical low, and eventually resulted in an unnamed hurricane (left).*

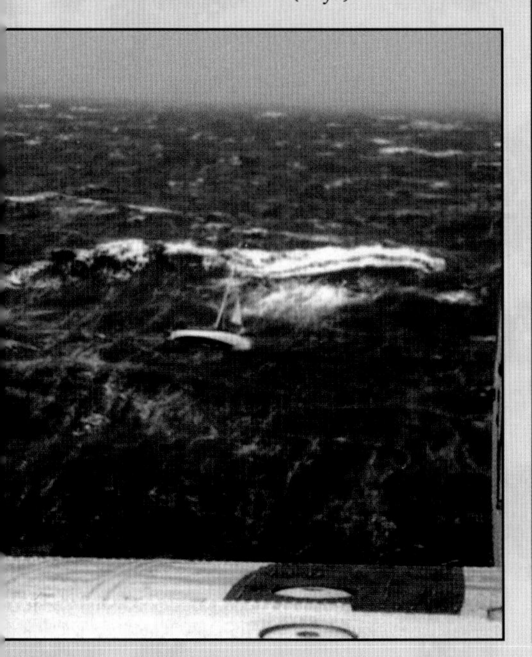

The Beaufort Scale

One of the first scales used to estimate wind speeds was created by Sir Francis Beaufort (1774–1857), a British admiral. He developed the scale in 1805 to help sailors estimate the winds using visual clues. A land version was also made. The Beaufort scale, which is still used today to estimate wind strengths, starts at 0 and ends at a force of 12.

A moderate breeze at 8–12 mph (13–19 km/h) is 4 on the Beaufort scale and is described as "Raises dust and loose paper; small branches are moved." A gale is at 8 on the scale with winds between 39–46 mph (63–74 km/h), and described as "Breaks twigs off trees; generally impedes progress." A hurricane has the highest rating of 12 with wind speeds between 73–83 mph (117–134 km/h). The entire scale is shown on page 46.

THE TRI-STATE TORNADO

...TO TOUCH DOWN THREE MILES (FIVE KILOMETERS) NORTHWEST OF ELLINGTON.

AT 1:14 P.M., THE TORNADO APPROACHES ANNAPOLIS FROM THE SOUTHWEST.
ROOOOAAAAR!
30 SECONDS LATER THE TOWN IS GONE.
AT 2:20 P.M. THE TORNADO CROSSES THE MISSISSIPPI AND ENTERS ILLINOIS. SO FAR ELEVEN PEOPLE ARE DEAD, 75 INJURED.
FIRST NATIONAL BANK, GORHAM, ILLINOIS, 2:25 P.M.
WHAT THE HECK IS THAT NOISE?
SOUNDS LIKE A FREIGHT TRAIN!

ERNEST SWARTZ HAS BEEN A BANK TELLER ALL HIS WORKING LIFE.
GET THE MONEY INTO THE VAULT! HURRY!
CRAASH!
HELP ME LOCK IT!
OUTSIDE ON MAIN STREET...
HOLY COW!

GOT TO HANG ONTO SOMETHI...HUH?
MOOOOOO!
WHOA!
CRASH!
THAT WAS CLOSE!
WHAANG!
OH NO...
CRACK!
AAAAGH!

THE PRINCIPAL'S OFFICE, WASHINGTON SCHOOL, MURPHYSBORO, 2:35 P.M.
BRNNG! BRNNG!
ER...LEAVE THAT PLEASE, THELMA.
LISTEN, EVERYBODY MUST GO TO THE BASEMENT-RIGHT NOW!
SINGLE FILE, HURRY NOW!
THELMA DAVIS IS IN THE EIGHTH GRADE.
OH MY, WHAT'S THAT IN THE SKY?

MEANWHILE IN GORHAM...

COUGH! COUGH! ERNIE? ARE YOU OKAY?

I THINK SO. SAY, DO YOU HAVE A LIGHT?

OH MY!
WHERE'S OUR TOWN?
THE HOME OF FRANCIS AND LOONY DAVIS, ELM ST, MURPHYSBORO.
OH NO! THERE'S A TWISTER COMING! WHAT DID LOONY SAY I SHOULD DO?
ROOAAAAR!
"OPEN THE DOOR TO RELIEVE PRESSURE ON THE HOUSE..."
CLICK!

AAAAARRRGH!
MAIN STREET, DESOTO, ILLINOIS, 2:38 P.M., THE TORNADO HAS GOTTEN STRONGER AND COME NEARER TO THE GROUND.
WHACK!
CRAAASH!
LIPSEY'S FARM, NEAR WEST FRANKFORT, ILLINOIS, 2:50 P.M.
I REALLY THINK IT'S TIME WE GOT IN THE CELLAR, MOM.

HANG ON SWEETIE, EVERYTHING'S GOING TO BE OKAY.
CAN'T DO ANYTHING BUT RIDE IT OUT.
THUMP!
CRASH!
WHUMP!

I THINK IT'S OVER. HERE–
UNNNGH! THERE'S SOMETHING BLOCKING IT!
THOSE TREES OVER THERE ARE UNTOUCHED, WE MUST HAVE BEEN RIGHT AT THE EDGE OF IT!
SO MUCH DEBRIS...
HEY! WHAT A LOVELY SCARF!

I WONDER WHERE IT CAME FROM?
ELM ST, MURPHYSBORO.
FRANCIE! FRANCIE? OH NO...
WASHINGTON SCHOOL.
WATCH WHERE YOU STEP, THE POWER LINES ARE LIVE!
THELMA?
WASHING
GRADE
SCHOOL

MOTHER?
IS THAT YOU?
PRINCETON, INDIANA, 4:16 P.M., THE TRI-STATE TORNADO HAS BEEN ON THE GROUND FOR OVER THREE HOURS, AND COUNTING...
ROOOAAAARUMMM!
RUN FOR YOUR LIVES!
MURPHYSBORO, 6:30 P.M., THE DAVIS FAMILY IS STAYING WITH RELATIVES IN A LESS DAMAGED PART OF TOWN.
I HEARD THE TWISTER FINALLY GAVE OUT AFTER HITTING PRINCETON AT 4:30.
TOO LATE FOR US, POP.

IT SEEMS AS IF ALL OF MURPHYSBORO IS ON FIRE TONIGHT.
WHAT I DON'T GET IS THAT THERE WAS NO FUNNEL CLOUD, SO NO ONE SAW IT COMING.
YOU'RE RIGHT, NO ONE HAD ANY WARNING...
...NO WARNING AT ALL.
THE TORNADO PLOWED A PATH OF DESTRUCTION 219 MILES (352 KILOMETERS) LONG. MORE THAN 2,000 PEOPLE WERE INJURED, 695 PEOPLE DIED, AND 15,000 HOMES WERE DESTROYED. METEOROLOGISTS PREDICT IT IS ONLY A MATTER OF TIME BEFORE A TORNADO OF THIS MAGNITUDE WILL STRIKE THE MIDWEST AGAIN.
THE END

THE HALLOWEEN STORM

THE GREAT SOUTH CHANNEL, OFF THE COAST OF MAINE, OCTOBER 26, 1991.

RAY, DID YOU CATCH THE WEATHER REPORT ABOUT THE FRONT THAT'S COMING IN?

U.S. NATIONAL WEATHER SERVICE, LOGAN AIRPORT, BOSTON, MASSACHUSETTS, OCTOBER 28.
WALT, IF OUR FORECASTS ARE CORRECT AND THIS LOW PRESSURE SYSTEM SOUTHEAST OF NOVA SCOTIA GROWS STRONGER...
...WE ARE GOING TO HAVE ONE HECK OF A STORM OVER THE ATLANTIC.
METEOROLOGIST BOB CASE IS IN CHARGE OF ISSUING LOCAL WEATHER BULLETINS.
IF THE WARM MOISTURE, FLOWING OUT OF THIS DYING HURRICANE TO THE SOUTH, GETS DRAWN INTO THE STORM'S SPIRAL–IT'LL BE LIKE THROWING GASOLINE ONTO A FIRE!
THE ATLANTIC OCEAN 44° NORTH 56° WEST, 2:00 P.M.
BEEP... TICKKA... TICKKA...

WARNINGS. HURRICANE GRACE MOVING E
5 KNOTS MAXIMUM WINDS 65 KNOTS
GUSTING TO 80 NEAR CENTER. FORECAST
DANGEROUS STORM WINDS 50 TO 75
KNOTS AND SEAS 25 TO 35 FT.
HMMM...
TICKKA...BEEP!
THE SWORDFISHING BOAT ANDREA GAIL IS CAPTAINED BY SKIPPER BILLY TYNE.
RIIIP!
STILL CALM...FOR NOW.
BELOW DECK...
TWO MORE DAYS, BOYS, AND WE'LL BE HOME SWEET HOME.
THEY ARE RETURNING TO GLOUCESTER, MASSACHUSETTS, AFTER A LONG MONTH SPENT FISHIING OUT AT FLEMISH CAP, FAR TO THE EAST.

6 P.M., EAST OF SABLE ISLAND.
MESSAGE TO THE FLEET. SHE'S COMING ON, BOYS, AND SHE'S COMING ON STRONG!
OTHER BOATS FROM THE GLOUCESTER SWORD FLEET ARE STILL FISHING 600 MILES (966 KILOMETERS) FARTHER EAST.
9 P.M., NORTHEAST OF SABLE ISLAND.
CRAAAASH!!
GNNNH!

HEY, WHAT HAPPENED, SKIP?
I THINK WE JUST LOST OUR RADIO ANTENNA.
BOBBY SHATFORD IS SECOND IN COMMAND.
AROUND 10:00 P.M.
THIS SEA'S GETTING TOO BIG, I'M GOING TO STEER HER AROUND– TAKE THE WAVES HEAD ON.

SWORDFISH BOAT, THE ALLISON, SOUTH OF FLEMISH CAP.
STILL NOTHING, HE'S EITHER SUNK, OR HIS RADIO'S DEAD.

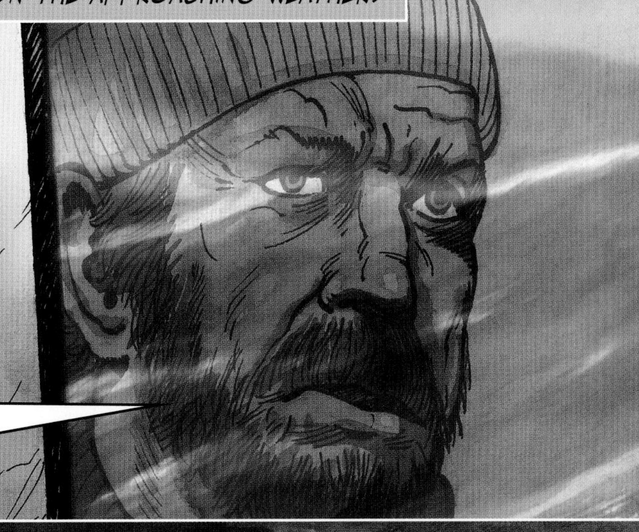
THE PREVIOUS DAY, BILLY TYNE HAD PROMISED TO UPDATE TOMMY BARRIE, SKIPPER OF THE ALLISON, ON THE APPROACHING WEATHER.
IT'S GOT TO BE BLOWING FORCE 12 OVER SABLE, WIND SPIKING TO OVER 100 MILES AN HOUR. 70 FT SEAS. HE CAN'T ENDURE THAT FOR LONG!

ANDREA GAIL, 10:30 P.M.
WHUMP!
AAAGH!

IT FELT LIKE WE HIT SOMETHING!
I'M GOING UP TOP!

AS SHATFORD OPENS THE BRIDGE DOOR...
CRASH!
UUUGH!
WINDOW'S GONE!
GET THE PLYWOOD AND TOOLS!
MEANWHILE SOME 600 MILES (966 KILOMETERS) TO THE SOUTHWEST...
RAY, I CAN'T RAISE ANYONE—THE RADIO'S JUST STATIC, I'VE GOT A BAD FEELING ABOUT THIS.

SUSAN, PLEASE, THIS STORM WILL BLOW OUT IN A DAY—WE CAN RIDE IT OUT!
WE'RE GOING TO HAVE TO, WE'RE TOO FAR OUT TO TURN BACK NOW.
ON BOARD ANDREA GAIL.
I'VE NEVER SEEN A SEA AS BAD AS THIS! DO YOU THINK WE CAN MAKE IT?
MAYBE! IF ALL THE HATCHES STAY ON AND WE DON'T GET HIT BY A FREAK WA....
WHAT?
OH NO!

ON THE SATORI.
WHUMP!
AAARRGH!
SUE, PREPARE AN EMERGENCY BAG, IN CASE WE HAVE TO BAIL OUT. I'M GOING TO TALK TO RAY.
YES! OKAY!
BILLY! WE'RE NOT GONNA MAKE...

CRASH!
THE SATORI, 11:15 P.M.
RAY? I THINK WE NEED TO...
OH NO! THE LIFE RAFT...
...IT'S GONE!

Satori...this is the Satori 39.49 North 69.52 West. We are three people...this is a mayday...if anyone can hear us please pass our position on to the Coast Guard...this is a mayday...
U.S. NATIONAL WEATHER SERVICE, BOSTON, OCTOBER 29, 9:00 A.M.
HURRICANE GRACE IS FORECAST TO MOVE NORTH TOWARD THE SABLE ISLAND STORM.
THEN THE STORM WILL BE CAUGHT BETWEEN THE DYING HURRICANE AND THIS INTENSE HIGH PRESSURE AREA OVER CANADA.

NOR'EASTERS USUALLY MOVE WESTWARD BUT THESE TWO WEATHER SYSTEMS WILL FORCE THIS STORM EAST...
...INLAND! I'LL ISSUE A WARNING TO THE COASTAL AUTHORITIES.
THIS IS A ONCE-IN-A-LIFETIME EVENT...ALMOST LIKE A PERFECT STORM...
AT 2:15 P.M., THE CREW OF THE SATORI IS RESCUED.
BUT THIS IS JUST ONE OF MANY DRAMAS THAT WILL UNFOLD DURING THE STORM. THE ANDREA GAIL AND HER SIX CREW WILL BE REPORTED MISSING. A NATIONAL GUARD HELICOPTER WILL CRASH INTO THE SEA AND ONE OF ITS CREWMEN WILL NEVER BE FOUND.

OVER THE NEXT TWO DAYS THE STORM LASHES NORTHEASTERN U.S. COASTLINES WITH A STORM TIDE OF MORE THAN 14 FT (4 M). STORM SURGES OF 5 FT (1.5 M) WITH 30 FT (9 M) WAVES PILED ON TOP.
WHEN IT FINALLY BLOWS OUT, THE STORM WILL HAVE CAUSED ALMOST $1 BILLION WORTH OF DAMAGE AND CLAIMED TWELVE LIVES.

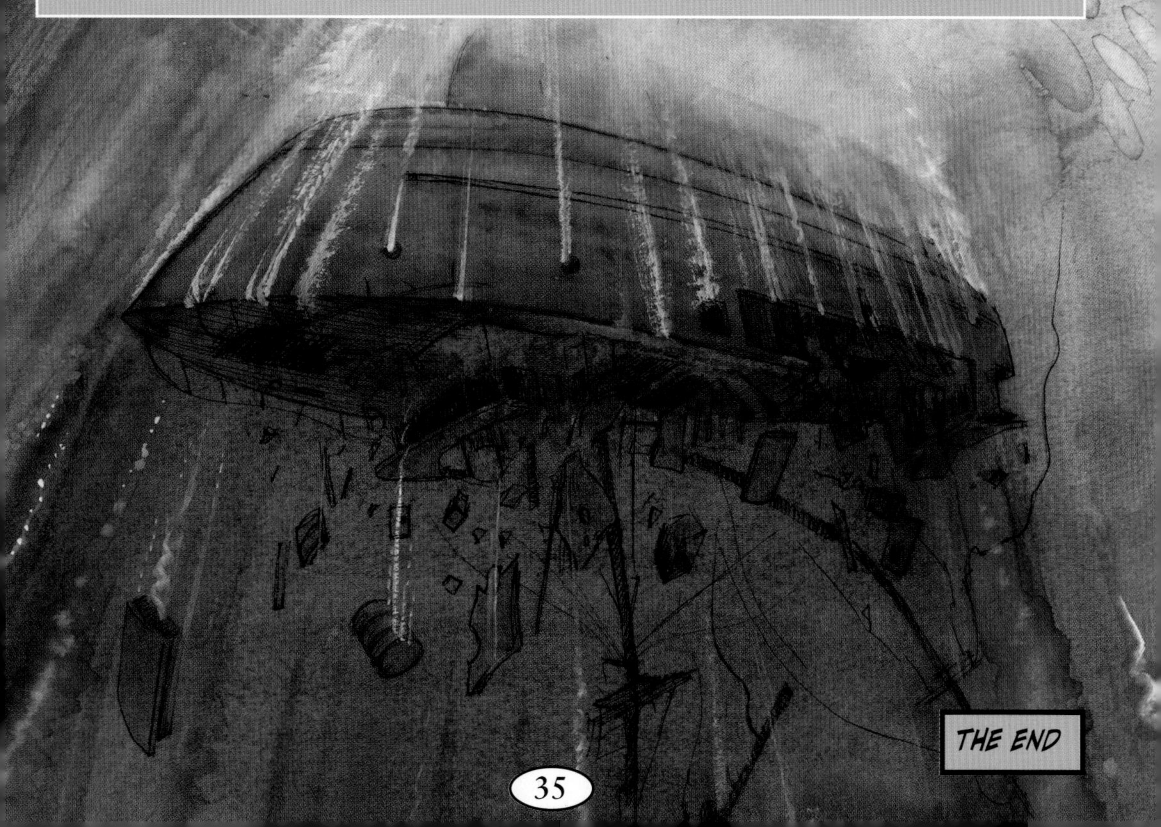
THE ANDREA GAIL HAS NEVER BEEN FOUND, IT IS BELIEVED SHE WAS OVERWHELMED BY THE EXTRAORDINARY SEA CONDITIONS CAUSED BY **THE HALLOWEEN STORM.**
THE END

THE JARRELL KILLER TORNADO

BELL COUNTY DISTRICT ATTORNEY'S OFFICE, TEXAS, MAY 27, 1997, 8:00 A.M.

HMMM...THIS WEATHER SYSTEM APPEARS TO BE INCREDIBLY UNSTABLE EVEN BEFORE BEING HEATED BY THE DAYTIME SUN.

ASSISTANT D.A. LON CURTIS IS A KEEN AMATEUR STORM CHASER.

LON CURTIS GOES HOME FOR LUNCH...AND CHECKS THE LATEST RADAR INFORMATION.

HOT-DIGGITY! THERE IS ONE HECK OF A SUPERCELL FORMING!

FIVE MILES (EIGHT KILOMETERS) NORTHEAST OF MOODY ON FM2113.
RUMBLE!
THIS IS A SEVERE THUNDERSTORM WARNING FOR THE WOODWAY AREA...
THE CHASE IS *ON!*
SOON...
HEEELLO!
WHIZZZZZZZ!
WHUZZZWHUSH!
CLICK!
GONE! BUT THIS IS JUST THE BEGINNING —I *KNOW* IT.
PHWWWIIIIP!

BELTON FIRE DEPARTMENT, BELL COUNTY, 2 P.M., LON CURTIS HAS JUST CALLED IN.
SO A THIRD TORNADO'S JUST ROPED OUT?
YEAH, BUT KEEP AN EYE OUT FOR DEVELOPMENTS IN THE LAKE STILLHOUSE AREA OR MAYBE EVEN FURTHER SOUTH AT SALADO...
PRAIRIE DELL, SOUTH OF SALADO, BELL COUNTY.
WHZZZZZWHUP!
HMMM...LOOKS KIND OF SKINNY...
HEY! WHERE ARE YOU GOING?
PHWHZZZZZZZZZZZUP!

LON GIVES CHASE, BUT...
I'VE LOST VISUAL!
VARRRROOOM!
WHAROAAAR!
WHAT THE?!–WHERE DID THAT COME FROM?
BELTON? CAN YOU NOTIFY JARRELL FIRE DEPARTMENT THAT A LARGE TORNADO IS HEADING STRAIGHT TOWARD THEIR TOWN!
VROOOOM!
JARRELL
5 miles

TONN'S FARM, 2 MILES (3 KILOMETERS) NORTH OF JARRELL.
EVERYBODY, IN THE CELLAR–NOW!
WHEEEEEEEE!
INTERSECTION NORTHEAST OF JARRELL.
WHAAAAR!
CRACKK!

JARRELL, 3:29 P.M.
ROOOAAAA
WHAT CAN WE DO?
UNLESS YOU'VE GOT A CELLAR TO HIDE IN -**NOTHING!**
OH MY LO...
LON CURTIS IS SOUTH OF JARRELL.
IT'S ACHIEVED WEDGE STATUS!
BUT WILL IT HIT THE CENTER OF THE TOWN?

AN F5 TORNADO WILL TEAR THE BARK OFF A TREE...
...TURN CAR-SIZED OBJECTS INTO MISSILES...
...STRIP THE SURFACE FROM A ROAD.
NONE OF THE HOMES AT DOUBLE CREEK ESTATES HAS A CELLAR.

THE NEXT DAY...
...ALTHOUGH THE CENTER OF JARRELL WAS MIRACULOUSLY SPARED, IT IS FEARED THAT 27 PEOPLE LOST THEIR LIVES WHEN THE F5 TORNADO TORE THROUGH NEARBY DOUBLE CREEK ESTATES SUBDIVISION.
Tornado Disaster
THOSE FIRST ON THE SCENE WERE UNSURE WHETHER A TORNADO HAD ACTUALLY BEEN THROUGH, BECAUSE OF AN ABSENCE OF LARGE DEBRIS PIECES ON THE GROUND.
THE DOUBLE CREEK SUBDIVISION...IT'S NOT THERE ANYMORE...IT'S BEEN WIPED CLEAN.
R B Raby
Deputy Sheriff
Chuck Tonn
Farmer
WE CAN ALWAYS REPLACE ALL OF THIS. IT'S JUST GOING TO TAKE A LITTLE TIME, BUT WE'LL BOUNCE BACK.
THE END

KEEPING A WEATHER EYE

Weather warnings for storms and tornadoes are becoming more accurate as the technology used becomes more sophisticated. Satellites, radar, and storm chasers provide valuable information to allow early warnings of approaching storms.

WARNINGS

A tornado warning is issued when a tornado is reported on the ground, a waterspout is heading toward land, or a funnel cloud is reported in the sky. The first tornado warning was issued by meteorological staff at Tinker Air Force Base in 1947. It was also the first successful tornado warning. Due to more advanced technology the death toll from tornadoes in the U.S. has been reduced from 1.8 deaths per million people per year in 1925 to only 0.11 deaths per million in 2000.

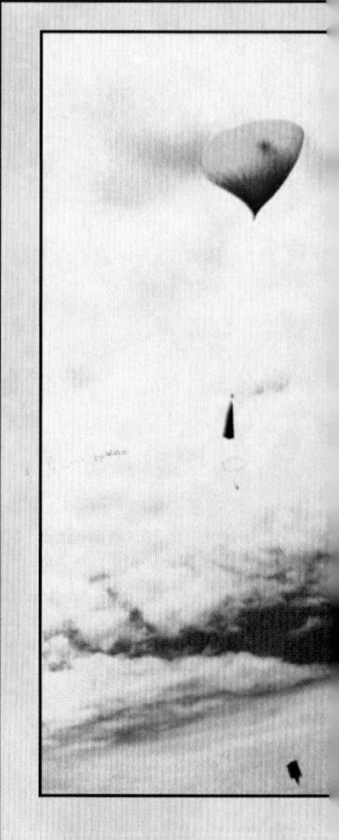

A team of "storm chasers" are the eyes on the ground (below). Their visual sightings of tornadoes are essential for tornado warnings.

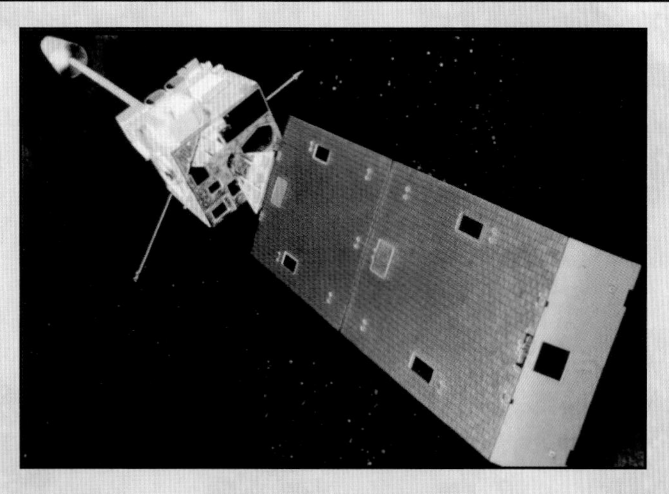

Weather balloons (left) can be sent up quickly to record valuable data on the atmosphere near a storm. Satellites provide a worldwide view of the current state of the weather. The GOES satellites (right) and NOAA satellites keep a weather watch for the United States.

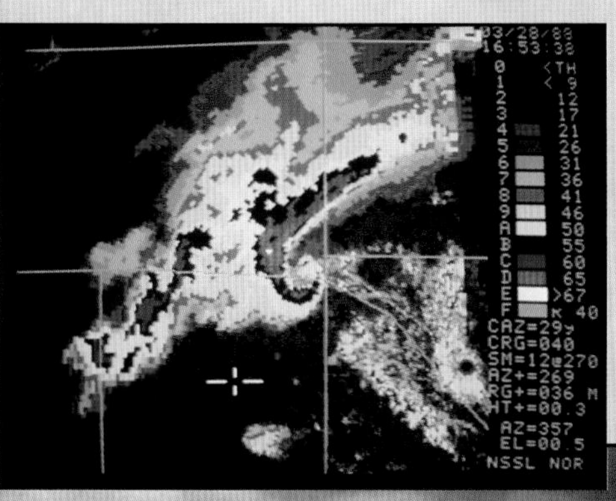

Information from mobile radar trucks (below inset) and weather radar stations (below) provide valuable insight into storm activity. Tornadoes can be predicted earlier by reading the signs, such as the "hook echo" on the radar screen (left), which is often a sign of tornado activity to come.

GLOSSARY

anvil A solid metal block used by blacksmiths to shape metal objects. It has a flat top surface, and is wider at the top.

asphalt A hardwearing, waterproof road surface made of small granules of rock held together with tar. It is also known as tarmac.

bulletin A short, regular news report.

extratropical low An area of low pressure that exists outside the tropical area. The tropical area is the space between the Tropic of Cancer and the Tropic of Capricorn.

knot One nautical mile per hour, which is one and a half miles (two kilometers) per hour.

low atmospheric pressure An area associated with strong winds that brings cloudy or overcast skies. These areas are often called "lows."

meteorological Having to do with the weather.

mid-latitude Horizontal lines of the areas between 30 and 60 degrees north or south of the equator.

radar (**ra**dio **d**etection **a**nd **r**anging) A method or device that detects objects, such as clouds, by sending out radio waves which are reflected back.

skipper The captain of a ship or boat.

static A hissing or crackling noise on a radio produced by radio wave interference.

storm surge A rise in the sea level, moving forward in front of a storm, which causes coastal flooding when it hits land.

supercell A severe thunderstorm that can produce tornadoes.

wedge A triangular shape.

THE BEAUFORT SCALE

	miles/hour		
0	**0–1**	**Calm**	Calm; smoke rises vertically.
1	**1–3**	**Light Air**	Direction of wind shown by smoke drift, but not by wind vanes.
2	**4–7**	**Light Breeze**	Wind felt on face; leaves rustle; ordinary vanes moved by wind.
3	**8–12**	**Gentle Breeze**	Leaves and small twigs in constant motion; wind extends light flag.
4	**13–18**	**Moderate Breeze**	Raises dust and loose paper; small branches are moved.
5	**19–24**	**Fresh Breeze**	Small trees in leaf begin to sway; crested wavelets form on inland waters.
6	**25–31**	**Strong Breeze**	Large branches in motion; whistling heard in telegraph wires; umbrellas used with difficulty.
7	**32–38**	**Near Gale**	Whole trees in motion; inconvenience felt when walking against the wind.
8	**39–46**	**Gale**	Breaks twigs off trees; generally impedes progress.
9	**47–54**	**Severe Gale**	Slight structural damage occurs (chimney-pots and slates removed).
10	**55–63**	**Storm**	Seldom experienced inland; trees uprooted; considerable structural damage occurs.
11	**64–72**	**Violent Storm**	Very rarely experienced; accompanied by widespread damage.
12	**73–83**	**Hurricane**	

FOR MORE INFORMATION

ORGANIZATIONS

National Oceanic & Atmospheric Administration (NOAA)
http://www.noaa.gov

Twister (the movie) Museum,
101 W Main, Wakita, OK 73771
(530) 594-2312

FOR FURTHER READING

Berger, Melvin, Gilda Berger, and Barbara Higgins Bond (Illustrator). *Do Tornadoes Really Twist?* (Scholastic Question & Answer). New York, NY: Scholastic, 2000.

Berger, Melvin, Gilda Berger, and Robert Roper (Illustrator). *Tornadoes Can Make It Rain Crabs: Weird Facts About the World's Worst Disasters: A Weird-But-True Book* (Strange World). New York, NY: Scholastic, 1997.

Galiano, D. *Tornadoes.* New York, NY: The Rosen Publishing Group, Inc., 2000.

Hopping, Lorraine. *Wild Weather Tornadoes.* Sagebrush, 1999.

Strain Trueit, Trudi. *Storm Chasers* (Watts Library). London, England: Franklin Watts, 2002.

Thompson, Luke. *Tornadoes* (High Interest Books). New York, NY: Children's Press, 2000.

Verkaik, Jerrine and Arjen Verkaik. *Under the Whirlwind: Everything You Need to Know About Tornadoes but Didn't Know Who to Ask.* Whirlwind Books, 2001.

INDEX

Web Sites

Due to the changing nature of Internet links, the Rosen Publishing Group, Inc., has developed an online list of Web sites related to the subject of this book. This site is updated regularly. Please use this link to access the list:
http://www.rosenlinks.com/gnd/tosu

EDISON TWP. FREE PUBLIC LIBRARY
3 9360 00618486 8